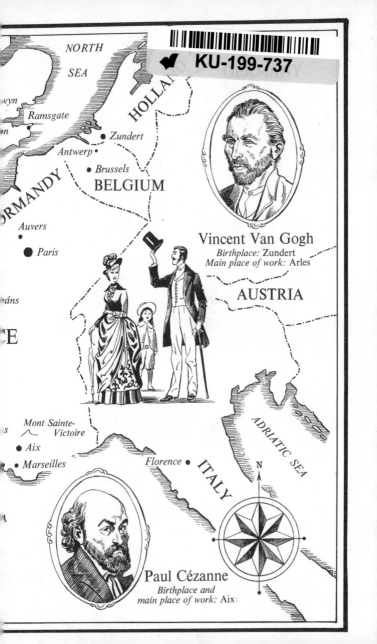

NORTH
SEA

HOLLAND

Ramsgate

Zundert

Antwerp

Brussels

BELGIUM

Auvers

Paris

AUSTRIA

Vincent Van Gogh
Birthplace: Zundert
Main place of work: Arles

Mont Sainte-Victoire

Aix

Marseilles

Florence

ITALY

ADRIATIC SEA

N

Paul Cézanne
Birthplace and main place of work: Aix

✔ KU-199-737

A Ladybird Book
Series 701

When one knows something of the background to the lives and characters of the great artists, and how their work was influenced by their environment, the pleasure of a visit to an art gallery can be greatly enhanced.

This book tells of the lives of Van Gogh, Gauguin and Cézanne, and a number of the full-colour illustrations depict them actually at work on well-known masterpieces.

Artists in this book :

VAN GOGH (1853-1890)

GAUGUIN (1848-1903)

CÉZANNE (1839-1906)

GREAT ARTISTS (BOOK 3)

by DOROTHY AITCHISON
with illustrations by MARTIN AITCHISON

Publishers :
Wills & Hepworth Ltd.
Loughborough
First published 1971 © *Printed in England*

Vincent Van Gogh (1853-1890)

Vincent Van Gogh was born at Zundert in Holland in 1853. His life was short and tragic, but his pictures are probably more popular than those of any other artist. His paintings, with their brilliant colour and vigorous brushwork, are reproduced everywhere. Exhibitions of his work are always eagerly attended.

Van Gogh's father was a parson, and his mother fond of drawing and writing. To the great sorrow of his parents, their first child died at birth, a year before Vincent was born. There were later to be five other children in the family.

Vincent was a strange and obstinate child, though he was affectionate. He loved nature, and his chief pleasure was to wander on the heaths and peat-bogs which surrounded Zundert, watching the farmers at work on their land.

Van Gogh was always fond of drawing, and he received a good education. At the age of eleven he was sent to school at Zevenburgen, and remained there for two years. He spent a further two years at another school at Tilburg, returning home at the age of fifteen. He was a solitary boy, with close-cropped hair, deep-set eyes and a stooping walk. At this time his main interest was in religion.

Three of Vincent's uncles were art dealers, and it was decided that he should follow their profession. In 1868, the young man was sent to work in the famous firm of Goupil, at The Hague.

4   *Van Gogh with his parents, leaving his father's church.*

0 7214 0280 1

Van Gogh worked for four years in Holland, and was then sent to work in Goupil's London branch, selling reproductions of paintings. He enjoyed life in the rich city, with its spacious parks and fashionable people. Here he lived very respectably, earning ninety pounds a year, but he was not to be happy for long.

He lodged in a boarding house in Clapham, and fell in love with his landlady's daughter—Ursula Loyer. However, she was already engaged and laughed when he proposed marriage. This upset Vincent so much that he changed from a considerate boy into a moody and difficult young man. His work suffered and he was transferred to the firm's Paris branch, but was soon dismissed altogether. One reason for this was that he would not try to sell pictures he himself did not like.

Nearly all Van Gogh's family had felt an urge to be of service to mankind, and Vincent was no exception. He decided to become a Bible teacher and took a post in a school in Ramsgate. His first task was to collect unpaid school fees, as all schooling had to be paid for in those days. Visiting the children's homes he was so overcome by the scenes of poverty that he returned empty-handed, and was dismissed from this position too. He then walked all the way to Welwyn in Hertfordshire, where his sister was a school-teacher.

His next idea was to become a clergyman or missionary among the English poor. With this end in view, he worked for some time with a Methodist minister, named Thomas Jones, in Twickenham.

At work at the art dealer's.

Van Gogh returned to Holland in 1877, and joined his parents who were then living at Etten. He resolved to enter the Church, and spent fourteen months studying Latin and Greek, but finally abandoned this ambition and entered a school for preachers in Brussels. He had a poor voice and was slovenly in appearance, so this venture also failed.

Van Gogh's last effort to serve the poor was in the Borinage, a very poor mining district in the south of Belgium. Here he lived in a hut and visited the sick. To help the wretched miners he earned a little money by copying pictures. He even gave away his clothes and all his possessions to help them. He became worn out by fatigue and deprivation, and looked so disreputable that he was dismissed by the Church Council.

At the age of twenty-seven, Van Gogh decided to serve mankind through art. He much admired the French painter, Millet, who painted scenes of peasant life and, as Van Gogh said, preached Christ's teaching. He visited several artists to seek their advice. His resolve to become a painter was followed by several attempts to obtain training in art. He worked for a while with his cousin Mauve, who was quite a well-known artist at The Hague. Mauve insisted that Van Gogh should work from plaster-cast models, but Van Gogh quarrelled with his cousin and smashed the models.

Van Gogh gives his overcoat to a poor miner.

Van Gogh once more joined his parents, who were now living at Neunen in Brabant, and was disappointed in love a second time when his widowed cousin refused to marry him.

By now he had begun to paint in oils, and his pictures were improving. His subjects were the peasants he loved so well, and his colours were dark and sombre. He felt that these people who toiled in the earth had great dignity. He made many studies for his picture—*The Potato Eaters*—which shows a group of peasants at their evening meal. He was now making discoveries about art, and the colours he used were slowly brightening.

In 1885, his father died, and Van Gogh left for Antwerp. His devoted brother, Theo, sent him money but still Van Gogh had to go short of food to buy painting materials. He saw pictures by Rubens, whose glowing colours finally made him give up his dark style of painting.

In 1886, Van Gogh joined the Antwerp Academy as a pupil, although he was now thirty-two years of age. He quarrelled, as usual, with the old-fashioned art teachers. He was still dogged by failure and, after a test, was relegated to the beginners' class, where the other pupils were thirteen-year-old boys. By this time, he had decided to join his brother Theo, in Paris, so he never knew how badly he had done in his examination.

A quarrel with an art teacher.

Van Gogh's brother, Theo, was a well-known art dealer in Paris and a patron of the Impressionist painters, who were active at that time. The Impressionists were open-air painters who tried to paint a fleeting impression of the light which bathed their subjects. They worked in flickering dabs of pure colour and were also influenced by Japanese print-makers. They worked mainly in the countryside near Paris, on the banks of the Seine and on the north coast of France.

Van Gogh met many of these painters, including Toulouse-Lautrec and Pissarro. He knew Gauguin and admired his work, and was introduced to Cézanne, who told him he painted like a madman.

He now began to paint in an impressionist manner. His pictures became lighter and brighter, and the paint was applied in rapid strokes. He was untidy and difficult to live with, but he had become a lively talker. His seriousness vanished and his paintings were bright and happy. In Paris he painted two hundred pictures, of which twenty-two were self-portraits; others were still-life studies, flower paintings and landscapes.

In two years Van Gogh overtook Impressionism and left it behind. He believed that a picture should do more than capture a fleeting impression.

In February 1888, tired of the gentle light of the Ile de France and longing for the brighter colours of the south, Van Gogh set out for the town of Arles in Provence.

Some of the artists Van Gogh met in Paris. Next to him— his brother Theo, then Paul Cézanne, Camille Pissarro, Paul Gauguin and the dwarf—Toulouse-Lautrec.

Van Gogh's dream of brilliant light and colour was to be rudely shattered when he arrived in Arles to find the countryside covered with snow. However, he settled down, and it is here that he painted the pictures for which he is so rightly celebrated.

As the spring advanced he painted the orchards in bloom and visited the Mediterranean at Saintes-Maries-de-la-Mer. Here he painted fishing boats on the beach. He took some rooms in a yellow house in the Place Lamartine, and worked extremely hard. In one year he painted two hundred pictures and made a hundred drawings. His own special style of painting developed at last, and he applied the colours with a system of dots and straight brush strokes. He made four paintings of the canal bridge at L'Anglois, and the famous studies of cornfields. Van Gogh's favourite colour was yellow, and he painted many pictures of sunflowers, and the famous *Yellow Chair*.

The local people of Arles sat for their portraits, and the Roulin family at the Café de la Gare each took their turn. Madame Roulin posed with her baby, and her husband was painted in his postman's uniform. Van Gogh's portrait of their son, Armand, in his yellow coat, must be one of the most popular portraits of all time. He painted himself, too, in a workman's smock and yellow straw hat. Never have so many world-famous pictures been painted in so short a time.

Painting boats on the beach.

Unfortunately, this spell of genius was not to last. Van Gogh was lonely and dreamed of bringing other artists to Provence. He wrote to his brother daily, and it was Theo Van Gogh who provided money so that Gauguin could join his brother in Arles.

Both men were poor and unsociable, and each found it very difficult to live in peace with others. Gauguin did not like Arles, which he thought was a small and petty place, and was also condescending about Van Gogh's painting. They soon began to quarrel, and Van Gogh threw a glass at Gauguin. He then followed Gauguin through the streets with an open razor. When Gauguin took refuge in a hotel, Van Gogh, in a frenzy, cut off part of his own ear and was taken to hospital. After recovering a little, he painted two beautiful pictures of himself with his ear bandaged.

Shortly after he left the hospital he became ill again, and the people of Arles were afraid of him. Eighty citizens signed a paper saying that he was insane. Van Gogh was forced to go as a voluntary patient to a hospital at St. Rémy, in Provence. Here he suffered from fits of insanity, but was often well enough to work. He was allowed to go out with an orderly, and he painted many pictures of the hospital grounds at St. Rémy.

Van Gogh's work was beginning to be noticed by dealers in Paris and Brussels, but he was too ill to enjoy his success.

A doctor dresses Van Gogh's ear during a stay in hospital.

VINC[E]
VAN G[OGH]

As a result of his illness, Van Gogh's pictures became less brilliant in colour and his style of painting changed. He began to paint writhing, coiling shapes and stormy landscapes with tormented trees and ominous skies. His brushwork became explosive and turbulent, and his pictures were often sad and empty, except for one lonely figure. Once, during a mental attack, he swallowed oil paint, and on another occasion he kicked an orderly, thinking he was a policeman from Arles.

In 1890, Van Gogh was sufficiently recovered to go to Paris. He spent three happy days with his brother, and then went to stay at Auvers, a village not far from Paris. Many Impressionist painters had worked there, and Van Gogh was cared for by a Dr. Gachet. He painted pictures of the doctor and his daughter, and some landscapes of the surrounding countryside, but these pictures were untidy and distorted. His powers were gradually declining; he was alternately moody and cheerful, and was inclined to drink too much.

Van Gogh's brother had always supported him financially, but now Theo was married, with a baby, and had less money. He was also in poor health. Perhaps Van Gogh felt guilty because he was a burden to his brother. Nobody knows exactly what happened, but one day after returning from a visit to Paris, Van Gogh went into a farmyard and shot himself. He was thirty-seven years of age.

In spite of having such a tormented mind, this artist left behind him some of the most joyous pictures ever painted.

Van Gogh at work on one of his last paintings,
a portrait of Dr. Gachet.

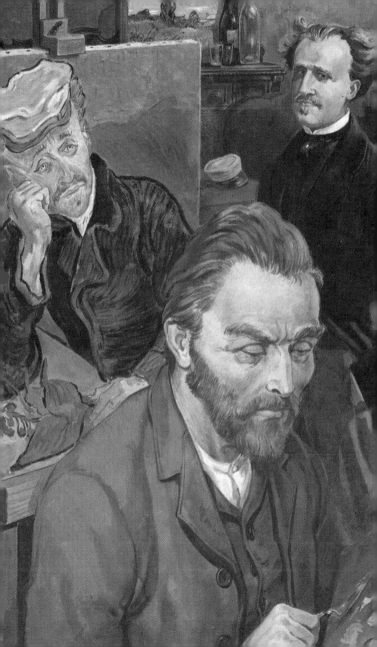

Paul Gauguin (1848-1903)

Paul Gauguin was born in 1848. His father was a journalist and his grandfather a grocer in Orléans. On his mother's side, his ancestors were rather interesting; his grandmother was the daughter of a Peruvian nobleman and she was said to be the descendant of an Aztec king. She was a very stormy person and wrote a book on women's rights. Her daughter—Paul's mother, was a modest and sweet-tempered person.

In the year that Gauguin was born, the family went to Peru. His father died on the journey, but his mother went on alone and was given a warm welcome by her family. Gauguin spent the first seven years of his life in luxury, cared for by Chinese and Negro servants. Peru gave him a taste for exotic surroundings and a liking for the art of primitive peoples.

When Gauguin was seven years old, his mother took him back to France to settle his father's family estate in Orléans. While she was away, her uncle in Peru died and her relations there squandered all the money which should have come to her.

Gauguin went to school in France, first in Orléans and then in Paris. His mother became a dressmaker. He was a dreamy and impulsive boy, who enjoyed carving toys out of wood. His school work was not outstanding, and when he wanted to join the Navy, he was unable to pass the examination to enter the Naval College.

Gauguin (on toy horse) during his early childhood in Peru.

Gauguin was, however, taken on as an apprentice on a three-masted schooner, and became a midshipman. He was a good sailor and showed no sign that he would later become an artist. He went on voyages round the world, and served on the Royal Yacht. This vessel became a warship in the Franco-Prussian War of 1870, and captured several German vessels.

Before his mother died in 1867, she had been wise enough to appoint a financier named Gustave Arosa to be his guardian. Arosa was a stockbroker and patron of the arts. He had several friends among the Impressionist painters. He placed Gauguin in a broker's office, and the young man became interested in a business career. In his spare time he collected paintings and copied pictures in the Louvre with his friend, Schuffenecker.

Gauguin was married in 1873 to Mette, a Danish governess who was working in Paris. He made money on the Stock Exchange and they lived in considerable style in a fine apartment.

In this apartment Gauguin set up a studio and painted in his spare time. He met the Impressionist painters and had a large collection of their pictures. His interest in painting was growing and, in 1876, he had a picture accepted by the Salon. He showed his work at exhibitions with the Impressionists, although he was not yet as skilful as they were and did not entirely agree with their methods of painting.

Gauguin serving as an apprentice on a schooner.

In 1883 there was a slump on the Stock Exchange and Gauguin lost a great deal of money. Always an optimist, he took very little notice and speculated unwisely. Shortly afterwards he resigned from his employment. He was now thirty-five years of age and the father of five children. He took his family to live in Rouen, where the cost of living was cheaper. His wife, Mette, was not very pleased; she had married a stockbroker whose hobby was painting, and now her husband was spending all his time on his pictures. In addition, he refused to reassure her about the future.

In 1884, Mette went back to Denmark with her children. Gauguin followed, but soon quarrelled with his mother-in-law. He returned to Paris, taking with him Clovis, his six-year-old son. There followed a terrible winter; Gauguin slept on the floor and they lived on bread and water. They suffered terribly from the cold and Clovis was ill. Gauguin was forced to earn a little money by working as a bill-poster.

Meanwhile, Gauguin was coming to maturity as an artist. He left the Impressionists because he was not satisfied with their ideas. He felt that a painting should do more than capture a fleeting moment. He believed that a work of art should convey some underlying meaning as well as represent reality. This, in fact, was the whole point of the Post-Impressionist movement, and the view was held by Van Gogh and Cézanne also.

Working as a bill-poster.

Gauguin decided to put his son in a boarding school and to move to Brittany, where a number of artists were working. Before long Gauguin had a considerable influence on them. His ideas were new to them, and his work was vivid and powerful. He paid four visits to the Breton countryside, but began to long for more exotic surroundings.

In 1887 he sailed to Panama, and worked as a labourer on the canal which was then being built. Here, amid fever and death, he worked twelve hours a day, shovelling earth. He was impressed by the beauty of the tropics, but became ill and was forced to return home. He painted a few pictures in Martinique on the return journey.

Although he was arrogant and quarrelsome, people were beginning to admire Gauguin's painting. In 1888, Theo Van Gogh, (the art-dealer) organised a successful one-man exhibition of his work. Theo knew that his brother Vincent was very anxious that Gauguin should go to stay with him in Arles, and to give Gauguin further financial assistance for the visit he purchased some of Gauguin's pottery.

Vincent Van Gogh had met Gauguin in 1886, and admired his work. He longed for Gauguin to stay with him, imagining that they would work together like brothers. The visit was not a success. Although they did help each other as artists, they argued bitterly. Gauguin dominated Van Gogh and was irritated by his untidiness and sentimentality. When Gauguin finally left for Paris there followed the scene we have already recounted (see page 16), when Van Gogh pursued Gauguin with a razor and which was followed by Van Gogh's total breakdown.

The mentally ill Van Gogh pursuing Gauguin.

We cannot hold Gauguin responsible for Van Gogh's breakdown, but there is no doubt that he was lacking in sympathy. When Van Gogh committed suicide, Gauguin was quite callous and considered his death a happy release.

Gauguin was sour and bitter when he returned to Paris and he was beginning to yearn again for tropical scenes. His work was becoming more decorative and symbolical, with black outlines and intense colour. He tried to raise money for a journey to Madagascar, but was unsuccessful. His patron, Theo Van Gogh, became ill and died soon after his famous brother, Vincent.

We can imagine that Gauguin did not arouse much confidence in art dealers. At the time he was described in these words: "A dark blue beret was permanently on his head, and draped around him he wore a long, beige ulster, now green with age. This covered a jacket decorated with splashes of paint and a navy-blue jersey appliquéd with Breton embroidery. His trousers were too long and subsided onto his wooden sabots with a curiously elephantine effect".

Gauguin himself may not have impressed the Parisians, but his paintings were attracting more and more attention.

His heart was now set on going to the South Seas, and he began collecting money for the journey. He had an exhibition and raised about ten thousand francs. He said goodbye to his children, who had not seen him for six years and were never to see him again, and in 1891 he sailed for Tahiti.

28 *Gauguin's appearance inspired no confidence in art dealers.*

Gauguin is regarded as a painter of idyllic pictures of the South Seas. He shows us the islanders seated among tropical vegetation, a mysterious timelessness about their poses and expressions. They show us the vision Gauguin had of a purer, more innocent world than could be found in the restless civilisation of Europe.

Unfortunately, the reality did not match this vision. The last Tahitian king had just died and the Society Islands were under French protection. Gauguin was bitterly disappointed with what he found, and particularly disliked the snobbish French officials. He much preferred the natives and learned their language and often dressed as they did. He moved from the main city, Papeete, to the south coast. Here he rented a hut which he shared with a Tahitian girl.

Gauguin worked hard, but could not forget his life in Paris. He also needed the wine and tobacco to which he was accustomed at home. Tahiti was not the answer to the problems of this tormented man, but while he was there he managed to come to firm conclusions about his own ideas of art. He believed that an artist should be inspired by nature and then paint according to his own inner feelings. Gauguin saw paintings as a flat surface, to be covered with colours arranged in a certain order. He thought that colour harmonies, rhythms and decorativeness were vitally important. He had a great influence on artists who came after him.

Gauguin in Tahiti.

Gauguin was restless in Tahiti and wanted to go to the Marquesas Islands nearby, where the natives were less corrupted by European life. His health was not good, and he suffered a heart attack in 1892. The following year he returned in a troopship to France, arriving with only four francs in his pocket. He soon received some money when an uncle died, leaving him nine thousand francs.

Gauguin held exhibitions of his work in Paris, Brussels and Denmark. The Parisians thought his style of painting was crude, but it aroused considerable interest.

Gauguin then settled in a studio in the Rue St. Vercingetorix, which he shared with a Javanese girl. The walls were yellow and decorated with axes, clubs and boomerangs. The artist dressed flamboyantly in a long-waisted, blue frock coat with mother-of-pearl buttons. He wore a green and gold waistcoat, grey felt hat with sky-blue ribbons, and white gloves. On a visit to Brittany he was so conspicuous that some sailors laughed at him. He became involved in a brawl with them and broke his ankle, which never completely healed.

On his return to Paris he found that the Javanese girl had left his studio, taking everything of value with her. Gauguin had a large sale of forty-nine of his pictures, and returned to Tahiti without saying goodbye to his family. He was never to see France again.

A Breton child raises the alarm after seeing Gauguin injured by sailors.

Gauguin did not like Tahiti any more when he returned in 1895, and he was disgusted to find the island lit by electricity. Again he aroused the hostility of the European community by building his home in the native district. This was a native-style dwelling of two rooms—"like a bamboo birdcage with a thatched roof of coconut fibre".

As he was always suffering illness, real or imagined, he ran up a large bill for medicine with the local apothecary. The apothecary said he would cancel the debt in return for a painting, and Gauguin worked hard to produce *The White Horse*. This is one of Gauguin's most easily appreciated paintings, but when the apothecary saw it he was angry. "But the horse is green!" he said. Gauguin told him that if at mid-day he half closed his eyes he would see everything bathed in a green light. The apothecary refused the picture, saying that he wanted one at which he could look at any time of the day with his eyes wide open!

Financial difficulties were ever present for Gauguin in spite of sales of his works in Paris, and he had to work for a time in the Post Office in Tahiti. His eyesight was failing, he suffered fever and had sores on his legs. He became depressed and felt persecuted, imagining his mail was being stolen, and was involved in quarrels and legal disputes. He even started to edit his own newspaper, with the result that he neglected his painting.

The apothecary rejects Gauguin's painting.

In 1901, life finally became a little easier for Gauguin. He felt he had at last exhausted the artistic possibilities of Tahiti, and he decided to settle on the Marquesas Islands where life was cheaper and more simple and the landscape less spoiled. He thought that, just as his Tahitian pictures had made his Breton paintings look dull, the pictures he would now paint would surpass those done in the Society Islands.

The dealer, Vollard, was sending him a regular income from the sale of his paintings in Paris, and his financial worries were over. Gauguin built a house on a volcanic reef, with a huge studio and shelter from the broiling sun. He was able to live in some comfort at last. Even here, however, he was continually quarrelling with the police and with the Catholic priests who had great influence over the timid islanders, but in his dealings with the natives he was always kind and gentle. He refused to pay his taxes, and encouraged the natives not to do so.

Gauguin was now fifty-five years old, but life in Tahiti had aged him and he suffered greatly from eczema. He was a strange sight in his native vest, his coloured loin cloth, his green beret with a silver buckle and his steel-rimmed glasses. He went barefoot and his legs were heavily bandaged.

He survived a terrible hurricane which hit the islands in 1903, but died soon after. His quarrelsome nature was soon forgotten, but his pictures survived to make him regarded as one of the founders of modern art.

Gauguin always remained an enemy of authority and a friend of the natives.

Paul Cézanne (1839-1906)

Paul Cézanne was born in 1839, in the quiet old town of Aix-en-Provence in the south of France. He was nine years older than Gauguin and fourteen years older than Van Gogh. His life was less stormy than theirs, and he outlived them both.

Cézanne was the son of a hatter who had bought a Bank and become a prosperous citizen of Aix. He was a stern parent and Cézanne feared him until he died. His mother was an uneducated woman, but she was interested in art and often told her son that he had the same christian name as the great artists Rubens and Veronese.

When Paul was five years old, he drew a bridge in charcoal on the wall. A neighbour saw it and said, "Why, it's the Pont de Mirabeau." In spite of this early recognition, Paul was by no means an artistic prodigy. He was quite clever at school, and won prizes for mathematics and science as well as for classics and literature. He also wrote poetry and played the cornet in the school band. He was a hot-tempered child, and remained quarrelsome all his life. His younger sister was the only person who could calm his rages.

Paul's family was not accepted socially by the important families in Aix, so their life was somewhat isolated. However, Paul had one friend who was to have a great influence on him.

The young Cézanne's first drawing.

After a period at boarding-school, Paul entered the Collège Bourbon at Aix when he was thirteen years old. It was the best school in Aix, and in the class below him was Emile Zola, who was destined to become one of France's greatest novelists. Paul and Emile became great friends and, strangely enough, it was Emile who won the prizes for drawing at school.

Emile's father was an engineer, who built a dam up in the hills above the town. During the long, hot days, the boys spent hours bathing in the pool behind the dam. They also wrote long poems together, or went hunting. From the dam, Cézanne could see the Mont Sainte-Victoire which he painted so often when he was grown up. In later life he also constantly painted pictures of people bathing.

As he grew up, Cézanne lost interest in all his work except drawing. He used to go whenever he could to the Free Drawing School in Aix. At first he failed his school examinations, but later managed to pass them. To please his father, he then began to study law.

At this time Paul's father bought a large house called the Jas de Bouffan, just outside Aix. It was a fine building with high ceilings, and stood among wild gardens at the end of an avenue of chestnuts. But Paul's father was interested only in the vineyards, and the mansion was very neglected.

In view of Mont Sainte-Victoire, which he later painted in many famous pictures, Cézanne bathed with Emile Zola.

Cézanne soon gave up any idea of studying law. He drifted about in Aix, mixing with other artists, and he decorated the walls of one of the gloomy salons of the Jas de Bouffan. At this stage his work was untrained and clumsy. He knew he should go to Paris to study, but feared to leave Aix, and his father was reluctant to let him go. He was urged by his friend, Emile Zola, to join him in Paris, and finally managed to persuade his father to give him an allowance.

In 1861, Cézanne arrived in Paris and enrolled at the Atelier Suisse. It was the custom for students to work from life models in the studio of some established artist, and so he studied in the afternoon with Villeneuve, a painter from Aix.

This first attempt to settle in Paris was a failure, and in five months Cézanne returned to Aix. He made a futile effort to settle down as a clerk in his father's bank, but he disliked banking as much as he disliked law, so his father sent him back to Paris to study at the Ecole des Beaux Arts. Unfortunately Cézanne failed the entrance examination to this famous school.

He then rejoined the Atelier Suisse and worked there every morning. In the afternoons he copied pictures in the Louvre. He was never able to settle permanently in Paris, and throughout his life he returned periodically to the quiet, sunlit city of his youth.

A restless Paul Cézanne could not settle to work in his father's bank.

At this period of his life Cézanne's work brought him nothing but discouragement. However he did make friends with a number of other artists, including the Impressionist painters Monet, Pissarro and Sisley, although he was never an Impressionist himself. At this time too, he formed an association with a young woman, Hortense Fiquet, but he was too afraid of his father to marry her.

When the Franco-Prussian war started in 1870, some of his friends joined the army. Monet and Pissarro went to England, whilst Cézanne avoided military service by hiding in the village of L'Estaque near Marseilles.

His painting began to improve and after the war he went to Auvers, the village near Pontoise where Van Gogh ended his life. There he became friendly with Dr. Gachet, who later cared for Van Gogh during his illness. Cézanne's struggle for recognition continued, but it was not until 1882 that he had his first picture accepted by the Paris Salon.

In 1886 his father died, leaving him sufficient money to free him from financial worries for the rest of his life, so Cézanne married Hortense and with a young son Paul, moved into the Jas de Bouffan. Visitors were sorry for him, seeing him work endlessly on pictures which they considered hopeless failures.

In that year also, Emile Zola published a book in which the main character, an artist who was a total failure, was clearly based on Cézanne himself. He and Zola were never again such good friends, though their life-long acquaintance was not completely ended. Cézanne was deeply hurt.

Cézanne going painting from the Jas de Bouffan.

Interest in Cézanne's painting was slowly increasing and his work was more frequently seen in exhibitions, but he was not understood by many people and had to endure scorn and mockery. Even Van Gogh, hardly an old-fashioned artist, declared that Cézanne's landscapes were the result of a wobbling easel. On the other hand Pissarro, Renoir and Degas, all established artists, were entranced by the "refined savage", as they called him.

It is interesting to consider his method of work. He was not concerned with spontaneous impressions or temporary effects. Instead he analysed the shapes he saw, breaking them down into the basic structures of spheres, cubes and cylinders. Having thus simplified the picture to a perfectly balanced geometrical framework, he would paint slowly, with little dabs of colour, starting with neutral tints and gradually strengthening the colour. He was a supreme colourist.

He took endless trouble to obtain his results. A sitter might have to pose over a hundred times for a portrait. When painting a still-life, Cézanne would spend hours arranging the drapery and fruit to produce a perfect composition. Perhaps he is most famous for his still-life paintings with apples. Truthfully he said—"With one apple I shall astonish Paris."

When he painted a landscape his eye sought out the forms of the rocks beneath the soil. His farmhouses became cubes and his tree-trunks cylinders. Later the Cubists followed his ideas and a new way of painting was born.

This slow, finicky, almost clumsy artist had an enormous influence on modern art, and to-day very high prices are paid for his pictures.

Cézanne enduring mockery and scorn at an exhibition.

By the time Cézanne reached his fiftieth year, his work was beginning to receive some recognition, and he was at last reaching the height of his powers. He could now afford to pay for models, and the gardeners and labourers of Aix posed for his pictures of card players. He was also able to hire a carriage so that he could go and make his beautiful water-colour drawings of the Mont Sainte-Victoire. His work was exhibited in Paris and Brussels and aroused the interest of many young artists.

Cézanne's home life was not particularly happy; his wife, whom he had married in 1886, was extravagant and his son was idle. Both preferred the gaiety of Paris to the quiet of Aix. He loved his son dearly, and one of his most famous pictures is of the boy and his friend dressed up for the Mardi Gras Carnival.

In 1895, Vollard, the dealer who sent money to Gauguin in Tahiti, held an exhibition of paintings by Cézanne. As usual, jeering crowds scoffed at his pictures, but experts bought them. Perhaps Cézanne was tired of being abused, and he did not attend the exhibition. He no longer met the Impressionist painters, and had no contact with the other Post-Impressionists. Van Gogh was now dead, and of Gauguin, Cézanne sourly re-marked: "He took all his sensations for a ride on ocean-going steamers. He has never understood me. He is not a painter but a maker of Chinese images."

Cézanne painting his son and friend
in Mardi Gras Carnival costume.

Cézanne's health was not good in later life. He suffered from diabetes but continued doggedly with his work in spite of his infirmities. In 1898 his old mother died and he sold the Jas de Bouffan. He built himself a modest studio with a fine view over the countryside of Aix.

The early years of the twentieth century were particularly successful for Cézanne. In 1900 he had three pictures in the Centenary Exhibition of French Art. In 1904 and 1905, he had many pictures exhibited in the Salon.

Dealers even went to Aix to buy pictures which Cézanne had given away to his neighbours. Vollard tells of a couple who found it hard to believe that they would receive a thousand francs for two of Cézanne's pictures. When they saw the money, the wife was so delighted that she included a piece of string to tie up the pictures. "Very good string," she said. "We wouldn't give it to everyone." Evidently she valued the string more than the pictures.

Cézanne was often lonely, and in spite of their earlier differences he was saddened by the death of his friend, Emile Zola, who died in 1903.

In 1906, Cézanne was caught in a sudden rainstorm while out painting, and later became very ill. A telegram was sent to recall his wife and son, but Hortense wanted to go to the dressmaker's and hid the telegram in a drawer. Cézanne watched in vain for his son, who did not arrive before he died.

The lives of Van Gogh, Gauguin and Cézanne were hard and often sad, but their work survives to give joy to countless millions.

Working on one of the many paintings by Cézanne of the Mont Sainte-Victoire.

WALES

ENG

ATLANTIC OCEAN

FRANCE
& WESTERN EUROPE

Concarneau

BRITTAN

F

Paul Gauguin
Birthplace: Paris
Places of work: Paris, Brittany
and South Seas

PACIFIC OCEAN
showing location of
Gauguin's South Sea Islands

ATLANTIC
OCEAN

Equator

Society Islands

Marquesas
Islands

Lima

PERU

TAHITI

PACIFIC OCEAN

SOUTH AMERICA

MEDITERRA

NEW ZEALAND